EARLY BIRD STORIES en español

Diversión con las hojas de otoño

Martha E. H. Rustad

Ilustrado por Amanda Enright

EDICIONES LERNER◆MINEÁPOLIS

NOTA A EDUCADORES

Al final de cada capítulo pueden encontrar preguntas de comprensión. En la página 23 hay preguntas de razonamiento crítico y sobre características del texto. Las preguntas ayudan a que los estudiantes aprendan a pensar críticamente acerca del tema, usando el texto, sus características e ilustraciones.

Muchas gracias a Sofía Huitrón Martínez, asesora de idiomas, por revisar este libro.

ediciones Lerner
Una división de Lerner Publishing Group, Inc.
241 First Avenue North
Mineápolis, MN 55401 EEUU

Si desea saber más sobre los niveles de lectura y para obtener más información, favor de consultar este título en www.lernerbooks.com

Las imágenes de la p. 22 se usaron con el permiso de: Mark Herreid/ Shutterstock.com (arce); MikhailSh/Shutterstock.com (pino); Maslov Dmitry/ Shutterstock.com (capullos).

El texto del cuerpo principal está en el siguiente formato: Billy Infant Regular 22/28. El tipo de letra fue proporcionado por SparkyType.

Library of Congress Cataloging-in-Publication Data

Names: Rustad, Martha E. H. (Martha Elizabeth Hillman), 1975- author. | Enright, Amanda, illustrator.
Title: Diversión con las hojas de otoño / Martha E.H. Rustad ; [illustrated by] Amanda Enright.
Other titles: Fall leaves fun. Spanish
Description: Minneapolis : Ediciones Lerner, [2019] | Series: Diversión en otoño | Audience: Age 5-8. | Audience: K to Grade 3. | Includes bibliographical references and index.
Identifiers: LCCN 2018028912 (print) | LCCN 2018029541 (ebook) | ISBN 9781541542662 (eb pdf) | ISBN 9781541540828 (lb : alk. paper) | ISBN 9781541545380 (pb : alk. paper)
Subjects: LCSH: Leaves—Juvenile literature. | Autumn—Juvenile literature. | Seasons—Juvenile literature.
Classification: LCC QK649 (ebook) | LCC QK649 .R8792518 2019 (print) | DDC 581.4/8—dc23

LC record available at https://lccn.loc.gov/2018028912

Fabricado en los Estados Unidos de América
1-45263-38787-9/17/2018

TABLA DE CONTENIDO

VIENDO LAS HOJAS

Vamos en busca de hojas de otoño.

Las hojas son coloridas en el otoño.
¿Sabes por qué las hojas cambian
de color?

Las hojas tienen muchas delgadas líneas. Se les conoce como venas.

Las hojas absorben
la luz del sol.

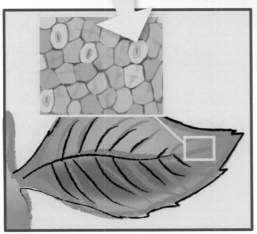

Respiran el aire a través
de pequeños hoyos.
Las hojas producen la
comida para los árboles.

Las venas transportan
la comida al árbol.

¿Qué hacen las venas?

CAMBIOS DE ESTACIÓN

Los árboles cambian
en cada estación.

En el invierno, muchos árboles no tienen hojas.
Los árboles no crecen durante los fríos días
de invierno.

¡**Mira!** Puedo ver un pequeño retoño en la rama.

La luz del sol durante la
primavera calienta los retoños.

La lluvia cae en el suelo.
Las raíces absorben el agua.

¡**Mira!** Puedo ver
una pequeña hoja verde.
Las hojas se abren
lentamente en los
retoños.

Durante el verano, la brillante luz del sol hace crecer las hojas. Las hojas son verdes en el verano.

En el otoño, las hojas dejan
de producir comida.
Su color verde desaparece.

Las hojas se ponen rojas,
anaranjadas y amarillas.

¿De qué color son las
hojas en el verano?

CAEN LAS HOJAS

Puedo ver una hoja cayendo.

En el otoño, el agua deja de
llegar a las hojas. La parte que
une las hojas a las ramas se
debilita. Las hojas se caen de
los árboles.

¡**Cronch!**
Las hojas muertas se secan
y se despedazan.

Algunos pedacitos de las hojas muertas
se hunden en el suelo.

Estos pedacitos son buenos para que las plantas crezcan.

Cuando las hojas se caen quedan pequeñas marcas en las ramas.

Cada marca es un retoño que se formó durante el verano.

Los retoños esperan todo
el otoño e invierno.
En la primavera, las hojas
comienzan a crecer otra vez.

¿Qué les pasan a
las hojas durante
el otoño?

APRENDE SOBRE EL OTOÑO

Durante la fotosíntesis las hojas producen comida para el árbol.

Los árboles de hoja perenne conservan su color verde y sus hojas—que tienen forma de agujas—todo el invierno.

Los pedacitos verdes dentro de las hojas se llaman clorofila. Producen comida para el árbol.

El color de sus hojas de otoño te dice qué tipo de árbol es. Los arces tienen hojas rojas o anaranjadas. Los abedules tienen hojas amarillas. Las hojas de los robles son en su mayoría marrones.

Las escamas de los retoños los protegen durante el invierno. Las escaman evitan que los retoños se calienten o se enfríen demasiado.

PIENSA EN EL OTOÑO:
PREGUNTAS DE RAZONAMIENTO CRÍTICO Y DE CARACTERÍSTICAS DEL TEXTO

¿Puedes pensar en otras plantas que cambian durante el otoño?

¿Qué les pasa a las hojas en el otoño donde tú vives?

¿Quién es el autor de este libro?

¿Qué significan los números en el índice?

GLOSARIO

marca: la huella que queda en una rama cuando se cae una hoja

raíz: la parte de una planta que se expande debajo de la tierra. Las raíces transportan el agua desde el suelo.

retoño: una pequeña parte que crece en una planta y que se convierte en una nueva flor, hoja o rama.

vena: un pequeño tubo dentro de la hoja. Puede transportar agua hacia la hoja y comida al árbol.

PARA APRENDER MÁS

LIBROS

Griswold, Cliff. *Fall Leaves.* New York: Gareth Stevens, 2015. Aprende más sobre los cambios en las hojas durante el otoño.

Schuh, Mari. *I See Fall Leaves.* Minneapolis: Lerner Publications, 2017. Lee más sobre las coloridas hojas de otoño.

SITIOS WEB

Villa de Actividad: Las cuatro estaciones
https://www.activityvillage.co.uk/four-seasons
Muestra cómo cambian los árboles en las diferentes estaciones en estas páginas para colorear y otras actividades.

ÍNDICE

Contents

Any words appearing in the text in bold, **like this**, are explained in the Glossary.

What are comets, asteroids and meteors?

The Sun, the **planets** and their moons are not the only members of our **solar system**. There are also billions of other lumps of ice and rock called comets, asteroids and meteors. These objects were left over from when the solar system formed about 4.5 billion years ago.

This stunning picture shows Comet Hyakutake, which blazed across our skies in March 1996.

This is a close-up view of the head and tail of Comet Hyakutake.

Comets

Comets are like dirty snowballs, made of ice, dust and gases. They travel around the Sun in long oval-shaped **orbits**. As they get closer to the Sun, the ice melts and a gigantic tail of gas and dust forms.

Comets are rarely seen in the sky. Fantastic ones with beautiful long tails appear about once every 10 to 15 years. More often they look like little more than faint, fuzzy 'stars'. Although comets travel very fast in space, they seem to move slowly across the sky over several nights because they are so far away.

Asteroids

Asteroids are lumps of rock drifting in space. They can vary in size from 1 metre across to being nearly a third of the size of Earth's Moon. There are almost 100,000 asteroids moving around the Sun, just between the orbits of Mars and Jupiter.

Only a couple of asteroids are bright enough for us to see them in the sky with our naked eyes. Even with a good pair of binoculars or a telescope, they are hard to spot and only look like specks of light.

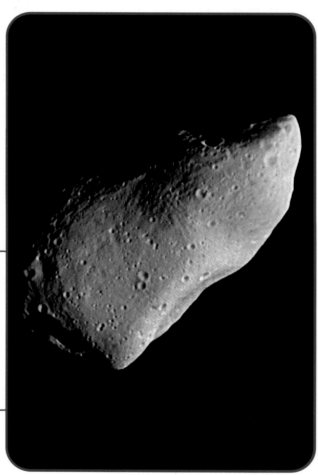

This picture of an asteroid called Gaspra was taken by the Galileo *spacecraft when it was only 5300 km (3300 miles) away from its surface.*

Meteors

Sometimes bits of dust or rocks from space come so close to Earth that **gravity** pulls them into its **atmosphere**. They then rub against the atmosphere and heat up. The lights we see are made by the incredibly hot pieces of rock burning. These fiery objects are called meteors.

The beautiful sight of a pair of meteors in the sky.

Meteors look like fast moving streaks of light in the sky at night. That is why they are sometimes called 'shooting stars' or 'falling stars'. They flash across the sky in just a few seconds, and can appear in any part of the sky at any time. Meteor streaks are common, and you can usually see a few every hour. Most look white, but red, yellow or even green meteor streaks have also been spotted.

During some months of the year many more meteors than normal can be seen. This is called a **meteor shower**, which can sometimes be like watching a firework display, happening out in space.

Why are they called comets, asteroids and meteors?

The word 'comet' comes from their flowing tails, and from the ancient Greek word *kometes* meaning 'long-haired'.

The ancient Greek word *asteroid* means 'like a star'.

The word 'meteor' comes from the Greek word *meteoron* which means 'a special event in the sky'.

Where do comets come from ?

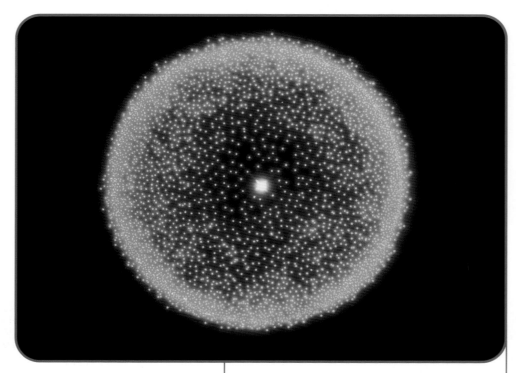

The Oort cloud is home to a huge swarm of comets, which surround the planets in the solar system.

Most of the comets we see in the sky start their journeys from a very distant region in space called the **Oort cloud**. The Oort cloud is in the furthest part of our **solar system**, further out than the **orbit** of Pluto. It is 15,000 billion kilometres (9300 billion miles) away, which is 100,000 times further away from us than the Sun.

There are many billions of comets in the Oort cloud, but they are all very cold, dead lumps of ice, dust and rock. Most of them are only a few kilometres across. There are also billions more comets that orbit the Sun, between Pluto and the Oort cloud. This second collection of comets is called the **Kuiper belt**.

Some fall toward the Sun

While they are in the Oort cloud and Kuiper belt, the comets are frozen, dark objects that we can't see. They don't glow, or have flowing tails. Sometimes however, a comet can get knocked out of these regions, perhaps by crashing into another comet. The comet's path is then changed, flinging it towards the inner part of the solar system because of the pull of the Sun's **gravity**. It then starts to orbit the Sun.

Their new orbits around the Sun are not circles like those of most of the **planets**, but long, oval shapes. These comets can take hundreds or even thousands of years to finish one lap around the Sun.

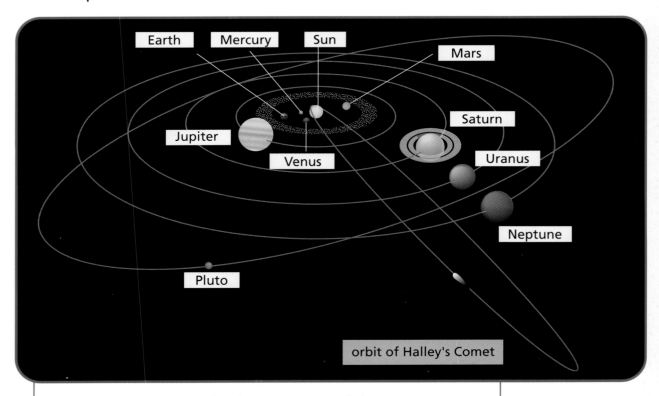

Earth · Mercury · Sun · Mars · Jupiter · Venus · Saturn · Uranus · Neptune · Pluto · orbit of Halley's Comet

The comets seen in the sky move around the Sun in very stretched, oval orbits. All the planets except Pluto move in circular orbits.

Why do comets have tails?

As a comet gets closer to the Sun, it begins to warm up. What started as a dark, frozen object turns into one so bright that we can see it from Earth. This change happens because the heat from the Sun burns off the ice on the comet's surface. The heated gases start to glow and the comet starts to squirt huge fountains of gas and dust into space.

Two tails

As the comet nears the Sun, the jets of gas and dust make enormous tails of material that stretch for millions of kilometres. At this time the comet can be losing more than 50 tonnes of gas and dust every second! It may now appear as a bright sight in our skies.

Comets have two types of tails. They have a **dust tail** made of **microscopic** grains of dust. A dust tail is not straight, but slightly curved. Comets also have a blue **gas tail** made of hot gas, which is straighter and narrower.

The tail of a comet always points away from the Sun. This is because it is being pushed back by a flow of electric **particles** blowing off the Sun. This flow is called the **solar wind**. The solar wind acts like a fan that blows the comet's tail away from the Sun.

Comet West was seen in the skies during March 1976. It has a narrow, blue gas tail and a wide, white dust tail.

The show must end

After many months, a comet will move around the Sun and head back into the outermost regions of the **solar system**. As it glides away from the heat of the Sun, the comet's surface cools down and starts to freeze over again. It returns to being a dark object, lost deep in space and no longer seen from Earth. It may be hundreds or thousands of years before that same comet returns to our part of the solar system and heats up again.

Comets weren't always liked

Comets in the sky have caused fear and panic through the ages. For thousands of years people thought comets brought bad news. This is because, unlike the Sun, Moon and stars, comets came and went without warning.

Comets have been blamed for many things on Earth. In AD 79, a comet appeared in the sky during the eruption of Mount Vesuvius, a volcano that destroyed the Roman city of Pompeii.

Some people, however, thought that comets were a good sign. After the death of the Roman leader Julius Caesar, many people were happy and they celebrated a comet that appeared in Europe in 44 BC.

The famous Bayeaux Tapestry shows Halley's Comet (upper right) in 1066.

11

What is a comet made of?

Apart from a tail, a comet has two other main parts called a **nucleus** and a **coma**.

The nucleus of Halley's comet as seen by the Giotto *spacecraft* in 1986.

Fragile nucleus

The solid part at the centre of a comet is called the nucleus. It may only be a few kilometres across. Unlike the **planets**, which are the shape of balls, it is an odd shape. The nucleus of a comet is made of loose dust and rock which is held together by ice. The ice is not only frozen water, but also frozen gases such as **carbon dioxide**.

A comet's coma

When the comet approaches the Sun, the ice in the nucleus starts to melt and gases begin to escape. This is when the nucleus becomes surrounded by a cloud of material called a coma. The bright coma can measure more than 100,000 kilometres (60,000 miles) across. That's nearly the size of the giant planet Saturn. The coma and the nucleus together make up the head of the comet.

The fuzzy spot in this picture is the growing coma of Comet Hyakutake, seen in March 1996.

Has anyone got really close to a comet?

A few **spacecraft** have been sent from Earth to fly very close to comets. One of these was the *Giotto* spacecraft, which flew to within 600 kilometres (370 miles) of Halley's Comet in 1986. *Giotto* discovered the comet had a potato shaped nucleus, 15 kilometres (9.3 miles) long and 8 kilometres (5 miles) wide. There were hills and valleys on the surface of the comet, with powerful jets of gas blowing out to make a tail.

Another spacecraft, called *Stardust* was launched in 1999 towards Comet Wild. It will collect dust from the comet in 2004 and bring it back to Earth for scientists to study. The material returned will teach us new things about what the **solar system** was made of when it formed billions of years ago.

13

Which are the most famous comets?

Thousands of comets have been discovered, but only a few of them are well known to us today because they were exciting to watch.

Halley's Comet

The most famous comet in history is Halley's Comet. It is named after the British **astronomer** Edmond Halley, who first worked out the comet's **orbit** in 1705. Although most comets are named after the people who first find them, Halley did not actually discover this comet. Chinese astronomers had seen it over 2000 years ago.

Halley's Comet passes through our skies every 76 years. It last appeared in 1986 and will return in the year 2062. Along its orbit in 1986, the comet came within 80 million kilometres (50 million miles) of the Sun, and passed 65 million kilometres (40 million miles) away from Earth.

Sir Edmond Halley (1656–1742) was a famous British astronomer.

Hale-Bopp

Comet Hale-Bopp was a magnificent sight in the night skies during 1997. At the head of the comet was a very bright **coma**, which was followed by two magnificent sweeping tails.

Millions of people watched Comet Hale-Bopp in the skies during 1997.

Hale-Bopp passed by about 197 million kilometres (122 million miles) away from Earth, which is nearly one and a half times the distance between Earth and the Sun. The comet was moving at a speed of 2 million kilometres per day (1.2 million miles per day). Sadly, Hale-Bopp takes so long to complete an orbit around the Sun that it won't be back in our skies for another 3600 years!

Comet Kohoutek

Comet Kohoutek was discovered in March 1973 by an astronomer called Lubos Kohoutek. He found it by accident, when it was still a long way from the Sun. There was a lot of excitement because people thought that when the comet got closer to the Sun and heated up, it would become the most fantastic comet seen for 100 years.

Although it had a beautiful tail, Comet Kohoutek stayed dim and never lived up to all the excitement. It won't return to our skies for another 75,000 years.

Do comets ever crash?

The surfaces of Earth's Moon and the **planet** Mercury have a very large number of **craters** on them. These are bowl-shaped holes that were made billions of years ago when comets or asteroids crashed there.

If it weren't for the wearing away or **erosion** of land by rain and wind, Earth's surface would also have lots of scars from crashed comets and asteroids. A few scars do still remain today. An 800 metre wide crater left by a crash 50,000 years ago can still be seen in Arizona, USA. Besides hitting planets and moons, some comets pass so close to the Sun that they get dragged in by its strong **gravity** and disappear forever.

A crash into Jupiter

In March 1993, **astronomers** discovered a comet called Shoemaker-Levy 9 which had broken into more than 20 small pieces, each about 1 kilometre (0.6 miles) across. The pieces of the comet passed so close to Jupiter, that the giant planet's strong gravity pulled them in.

The Barringer Crater in Arizona, USA is about 200 metres deep and 800 metres wide and was made when a huge rock crashed into Earth.

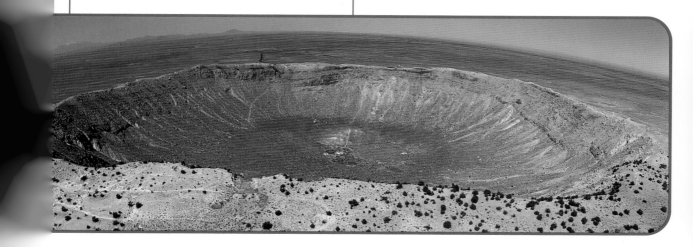

Dark, Earth-sized patches were seen in the atmosphere of Jupiter after pieces of a comet crashed there.

The broken up comet finally crashed into Jupiter between 16 July and 22 July 1994. The lumps of rock and ice thumped into Jupiter's **atmosphere**, and exploded in huge fireballs. They left large dark blotches made of gas and dust in the upper layers of Jupiter's atmosphere. These scars were the size of Earth, and could be seen on the surface of Jupiter for more than a year.

What killed the dinosaurs?

One of the great mysteries about the dinosaurs is why they died out so suddenly. Most scientists think that the dinosaurs died when a large comet or asteroid slammed into Earth about 65 million years ago. The object was about 10 kilometres (6 miles) wide and was travelling a hundred times faster than a bullet, when it crashed close to Mexico in Central America.

There was a huge explosion due to the crash, and it sent huge amounts of dust up into the atmosphere. The dust blocked out the light of the Sun for many months. Earth got cooler, the rains became poisonous, there were lots of fires, and the plants died. The dinosaurs became **extinct** around this time because they could not survive all these changes to the planet.

What are asteroids and where do they come from?

Asteroids are lumps of rock that were left over after the Sun and **planets** were made about 4.5 billion years ago. There may be over 10,000 asteroids larger than 100 kilometres (60 miles) across in the **solar system**, and many millions of smaller ones. Although asteroids are mainly made of rocks, dust and water ice, they also contain metals such as iron and nickel.

The main belt

Most of these ancient rocks are found **orbiting** the Sun between the planets Mars and Jupiter. This is the home of almost 100,000 asteroids, and the region is called the **Asteroid Belt**. The largest asteroid in this belt is Ceres. It is 950 kilometres (590 miles) across, which is almost a quarter of the size of Earth's Moon. Most of the rest of the objects in the Asteroid Belt are less than 1 kilometre (0.6 miles) across.

Jupiter is the largest planet in the solar system, and **astronomers** think that the strong pull of its **gravity** stopped all the asteroids in the Asteroid Belt gathering together to make another Earth-sized planet.

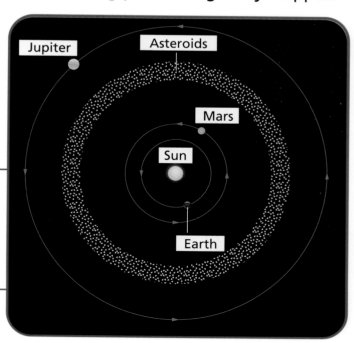

Most of the asteroids in our solar system are in a belt between the orbits of Mars and Jupiter.

Getting really close to asteroids

Most asteroids are too small and faint for us to learn much about them from Earth, even with very large telescopes. Over the past few years, we have discovered more about asteroids by sending **spacecraft** to visit them.

While on its journey to the giant planet Jupiter, a spacecraft called *Galileo* gave us our first close-up view of an asteroid. Between 1991 and 1993 it flew past the rocky objects called Gaspra and Ida. In 1997 the NEAR (Near Earth Asteroid Rendezvous) *Shoemaker* spacecraft passed close by an odd-shaped boulder called Mathilde. *Shoemaker* then went on to become the first spacecraft to ever go into orbit around an asteroid, when it circled Eros in 2000. A year later it actually landed on Eros, but it stopped working soon after.

The Galileo *spacecraft took this picture of asteroid Ida and its tiny moon Dactyl.*

19

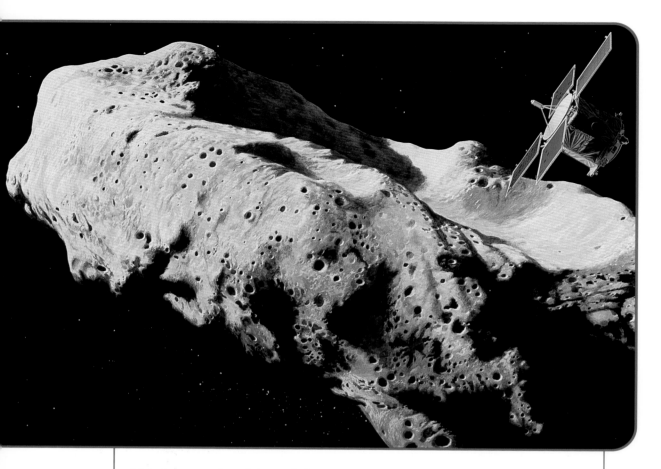

This is an artist's idea of the NEAR (Near Earth Asteroid Rendezvous) spacecraft orbiting the asteroid Eros.

Piles of rubble

The excellent pictures sent back by **spacecraft** like *Galileo* and *NEAR* showed us that asteroids are rocky objects with lots of **craters** on their surface. Amazingly, they also found that many asteroids are not solid, but seem to be made of several pieces. They are more like loosely glued piles of rubble and pebbles.

Another surprise was that the craters on some asteroids are very large. Mathilde is only 66 kilometres (40 miles) long, but it has a crater that is almost 30 kilometres (18 miles) wide and 6 kilometres (3.7 miles) deep. A smaller asteroid crashing into Mathilde caused this crater.

This was one of the last pictures sent back by the NEAR spacecraft, when it was 1.2 kilometres above the surface of Eros.

Could I visit an asteroid?

You could land on an asteroid, but there would be no air to breathe and no water to drink. The surface would be hilly, with lots of craters and ditches. It would take you less than an hour to walk all around a typical asteroid in the Asteroid Belt. Since most asteroids are so small, their **gravity** is very weak. This means you would feel very lightweight standing on the surface. A normal adult would weigh as little as a couple of spoonfuls of sugar on Eros.

Why do we need to study asteroids?

Most asteroids are safely tucked away in the **Asteroid Belt** between Mars and Jupiter. However, some have strayed out of this region and have ended up much closer to Earth.

Scientists keep a close watch on these stray asteroids. This is because their **orbits** around the Sun bring them so close to us that there is a chance that one might smash into our **planet**. An area of thick forest, almost 40 kilometres (25 miles) across in Siberia, Russia, was destroyed in 1908 when an asteroid exploded there. Luckily no one was killed.

A huge area of forest was destroyed in Russia when an asteroid exploded there in 1908.

If an asteroid the size of a football stadium smashed into one of Earth's oceans, it would make huge waves that could destroy cities along the coasts. A crash from a 10 kilometre (6 mile) wide asteroid or comet would be a threat to almost all life on our planet.

This is an artist's idea of a giant asteroid smashing into Earth. If this impact happened today, it could destroy all life on our planet.

No need to panic

There is no need to panic. The chances of an asteroid actually hitting Earth are very small. No asteroid or comet is known to be heading towards us today, but we do need to keep a lookout. There are more than 100,000 asteroids, each the size of a football stadium that could pass close to Earth. All around the world **astronomers** use telescopes to watch these asteroids. This way they can work out if any of them might be a danger to us.

What could be done?

In the very unlikely event that scientists discover an asteroid in space heading towards Earth, we will hopefully know about it many years before it gets close. There would then be enough time to launch rockets to the asteroid, and set off huge explosions above its surface. The force of the explosions would change the asteroid's orbit slightly, making it miss Earth and so keep us safe.

What's the difference between meteors and meteorites?

The **solar system** is littered with lots of small rocks and bits of dust. As Earth moves in its **orbit** around the Sun, these objects strike the **planet**. They heat up by rubbing against the planet's **atmosphere**. This is called **friction** and it works in the same way that you can warm up your hands by rubbing them against each other.

The smaller objects from space heat up and burn completely in the atmosphere. They leave behind the flashing lights in the sky called meteors. Anything between the size of dust grains, to a few centimetres across, will be too small to survive the journey through the atmosphere to Earth's surface. They will completely burn up as meteors.

Some scientists think that this meteorite, found in Antarctica in 1984, was blasted from the surface of Mars about 3.5 billion years ago.

Chunks that land

Some chunks of material approaching our planet from space are large enough to survive the scorching trip through Earth's atmosphere. Pieces that land on our planet's surface are called **meteorites**. They are usually just a few centimetres across when they land.

Three or four meteorites hit Earth every day. Luckily, very few people have ever been struck or hurt by a meteorite.

These scientists are collecting meteorites on the icy surface of Antarctica.

Finding meteorites is important because they are very old objects. This means that scientists can use them to learn more about the solar system when it was first made, billions of years ago. Most meteorites are pieces of broken up comets or asteroids. Amazingly, some have even been blasted from Mars or the Moon and have crashed on to Earth. Antarctica, near Earth's **South Pole**, is a good place for finding meteorites. They are dark and easy to spot against the bright, white ice.

Most meteorites are made of stone or rock. A few are made of metals like iron, and a tiny number are a mixture of stone and iron.

What are meteor showers?

If you look at a dark, starry sky, you will sometimes see streaks or flashes of light. These are meteors and you can usually see two or three of them every hour, every night.

Free firework displays

During some months of the year, many more meteors than normal can be seen at night. Perhaps as many as 100 meteors per hour may streak across the skies, looking like firework displays. These 'displays' are called **meteor showers**. One of the greatest meteor showers ever seen was on 12 November, 1833. People living in Europe and the USA saw almost 100 meteors every second!

Burning comet dust

Comets that pass close to Earth leave behind huge clouds of tiny dust grains. The material is spread in space, all through the **orbit** of the comet.

This Perseid meteor trail was photographed in Finland. The Perseids are meteors that are usually seen around 12 August each year.

Meteor showers happen when Earth passes through these clouds of leftover comet dust. At this time, lots of dust grains crash into Earth's **atmosphere** and burn up as bright streaks of light.

The meteor shower ends when Earth has completely passed through the dust cloud. We then have to wait a few months for the next meteor shower, when Earth comes across the dust of another comet.

Showers to look out for

Most meteor showers seem to start from single points in the sky, and streak out like exploding fireworks. The showers are named after the **constellation** of stars from which they seem to spread out. The displays are much easier to see in dark areas away from city lights.

The best meteor showers that you can look out for every year in the **northern hemisphere** are the Quadrantis shower 1–5 January, the Perseids shower 10–15 August, the Leonids 14 – 20 November, and the Geminids 10–19 December. The Perseids, Leonids and Geminids showers can also be seen every year from Australia and other countries in the **southern hemisphere**.

A Leonids meteor shower seen in 1999.

Fact file

Here are some interesting facts about comets, asteroids and meteors:

- The **Oort cloud** where most comets come from, is 15,000 billion kilometres (9300 billion miles) away. A **spacecraft** that takes 35 years to reach the furthest **planet** of the **solar system** Pluto, would take 90,000 years to get to the Oort cloud.

- The dust grains that burn during the Perseids meteor shower, every August, were left behind by a comet that passed close to Earth in 1862. The dust grains that burn during the Leonids meteor shower, every November, were left behind by a comet called Tempel-Tuttle.

- The **Asteroid Belt**, where most of the asteroids are found, is about 3 times further away from the Sun than Earth.

- For two centuries the largest known asteroid was Ceres, which is 950 kilometres (590 miles) across. In 2001 an icy rock called 2001 KX76 was found beyond Pluto. It is 1200 kilometres (745 miles) across, which is almost half the size of the smallest planet, Pluto. It now holds the record as the largest known asteroid in the solar system.

A bright, glowing comet can be one of the most fantastic sights of nature.

An artist's idea of the Rosetta Lander probe on the surface of Comet Wirtanen.

- Comets move through space at a speed of about 100,000 kilometres per hour (60,000 miles per hour).

- Meteors enter Earth's **atmosphere** at a speed of 100,000 kilometres per hour (60,000 miles hour). After being slowed down by the **friction** of the atmosphere, a **meteorite** may still be moving at 5000 kilometres per hour (3000 miles per hour) when it strikes the ground.

- In 2003, the European Space Agency will launch the *Rosetta* spacecraft towards a comet called Wirtanen. It will land on the comet in 2013 to study its surface.

Numbers
One thousand is written as 1000. One million is 1,000,000 and one billion is 1,000,000,000.

Glossary

Asteroid Belt doughnut-shaped collection of asteroids found between the orbits of Mars and Jupiter

astronomer scientist who studies objects in space, such as planets and stars

atmosphere layers of gases that surround a planet

carbon dioxide gas contained in Earth's atmosphere

coma large blob of gas that surrounds the nucleus of a comet as it gets close to the Sun

constellation imaginary pattern or picture formed in the sky by a group of stars

craters bowl-shaped holes made on the surface of a planet or moon by a rocky object crashing from space

dust tail part of a comet's tail made up of tiny dust grains

erosion wearing away

extinct no longer living, such as an animal species that has died out

friction force between two objects when they rub against each other

gas tail part of a comet's tail that is made up of gas

gravity force that pulls all objects towards the surface of Earth or any other planet, moon or star

Kuiper belt region beyond Pluto that scientists think contains large numbers of comets

meteorites bits of material that enter Earth from space and fall to the ground

meteor showers events during certain times of the year when many meteors can be seen every hour

microscopic something extremely tiny that can only be seen using a microscope

northern hemisphere the half of Earth between the North Pole and the equator

nucleus centre of an object, such as a comet

Oort cloud huge group of rocks and dust that surround the solar system. This is the home of most comets.

orbit path taken by an object as it moves around another body (planet or star). The Moon follows an orbit around the Earth.

particle very small piece, or amount, of an object or material

planet large object (for example, Earth) moving around a star (for example, the Sun)

solar system group of nine planets and other objects orbiting the Sun

solar wind steady stream of material given off by the Sun

southern hemisphere the half of Earth between the South Pole and the equator

South Pole point due south that marks the end of an imaginary line, called an axis, about which a planet spins

spacecraft man-made vehicle that travels beyond Earth and into space

Further reading

Exploring the Solar System: Asteroids, Comets & Meteors, Giles Sparrow (Heinemann Library, 2001)
How the universe works, Heather Couper and Nigel Henbest (Dorling Kindersley, 1999)

Index